# VILLAGE OF VAMPIRES

## Steven Otfinoski

A Pacemaker® Book

**FEARON/JANUS**
Belmont, California

Simon & Schuster Supplementary Education Group

# The PACEMAKER BESTSELLERS

## Bestsellers I

| | |
|---|---|
| Diamonds in the Dirt | Flight to Fear |
| Night of the Kachina | The Time Trap |
| The Verlaine Crossing | The Candy Man |
| Silvabamba | Three Mile House |
| The Money Game | Dream of the Dead |

## Bestsellers II

| | |
|---|---|
| Black Beach | The Demeter Star |
| Crash Dive | North to Oak Island |
| Wind Over Stonehenge | So Wild a Dream |
| Gypsy | Wet Fire |
| Escape from Tomorrow | Tiger, Lion, Hawk |

## Bestsellers III

| | |
|---|---|
| Star Gold | The Animals |
| Bad Moon | Counterfeit! |
| Jungle Jenny | Night of Fire and Blood |
| Secret Spy | Village of Vampires |
| Little Big Top | I Died Here |

## Bestsellers IV

| | |
|---|---|
| Dares | The Cardiff Hill Mystery |
| Welcome to Skull Canyon | Tomorrow's Child |
| Blackbeard's Medal | Hong Kong Heat |
| Time's Reach | Follow the Whales |
| Trouble at Catskill Creek | A Changed Man |

Series director: Robert G. Bander

Designer: Richard Kharibian

Cover designer and illustrator: Chris Kenyon

ISBN-0-8224-5370-3

Library of Congress Catalog Card Number: 78-72334

Printed in the United States of America.

10 9 8 7

# CONTENTS

CHAPTER **1**
## EMPTY VILLAGE

Sweat streamed down Paul Ross's face. His brown hair was wet. As he walked, he looked up at the hot Mexico sun. Then he looked down at his tired feet. Clouds of dust moved from the ground to the sky. The dust looked like smoke from a hot engine. Paul wiped his eyes.

"How far are we from Taxacola, Doc?" he asked the old man who walked beside him.

"Not far at all," answered Dr. John Lawrence. He took his pipe out of his mouth. "The village should be just over this hill." The doctor's red face had laugh lines. No matter what happened, he tried to smile.

"I hope they have a big dinner ready for us," said Sandy Lawrence, the doctor's daughter. She had been named well. Her long hair was the color of golden sand, caught by the yellow sun.

"Forget the dinner," said Paul. "All I want is a soft bed to sleep in."

Dr. Lawrence laughed. "Well, while you two are eating and sleeping, I'll be busy finding out what's going on in Taxacola."

The doctor had been to Taxacola before. It had been just over a year ago. At that time he had heard some strange news in his office in the United States. For years, vampire bats had been killing cows in Taxacola. The cows had died of disease spread by bat bites.

Life had been very hard for the people of the village. Their cry for help had been heard all over the world. But no one could help them. No one, that is, but Dr. Lawrence. When he heard of the sad story, he went right to the village. He made a special serum that he shot into the cows' blood. The serum didn't hurt the cows. But it did hurt the bats.

When the bats bit the cows and drank their blood, it killed them. Soon all the vampire bats in Taxacola were dead, and the doctor returned to the United States.

Then, just two weeks ago, Dr. Lawrence had gotten a letter from Hernando. Hernando was leader of Taxacola. The letter said that cows were being killed once again. Hernando asked the doctor to come back and find out why.

"Do you think more vampire bats have come to Taxacola?" Paul asked Dr. Lawrence as they climbed up the hill.

"It's possible," the doctor told his young helper. "And that's why I've brought more serum with me. Maybe the cows need more shots. Maybe the serum wears off after a while."

Sandy, Paul, and Dr. Lawrence kept on walking. Soon they stood on top of the hill. Down below them the tiny village looked like a painting.

"It hasn't changed a bit since I last saw it," said Dr. Lawrence.

"It looks dead," Paul said. "Where are all the people?"

"They're probably resting—having their *siesta*," answered Sandy. "They go inside and sleep when the sun is hot."

"Yes, but it's a little late in the day for that," said her father. "Come. Let's see what's happening."

They went down into the village. All was very still.

"Hello!" Paul cried. "Anyone home?" The only answer came from the blowing wind.

Dr. Lawrence opened the door to a house and looked inside. Then he opened a door to another house.

"That's strange," he said. "Everything is here. Not one thing seems out of place or missing. Yet there are no people."

"It's as if they all got up at once and left," said Sandy.

"But where did they go—and why?" asked Paul.

"There must be some good reason," said the doctor. "People who have lived in one place for hundreds of years just don't walk away. Let's look some more."

They walked into a field just outside the village. The field was very full of growing vegetables.

"They didn't even pick their vegetables before they left," said Dr. Lawrence. "These vegetables are going bad."

"You'd think they would take some food with them," said Paul. "That is, unless. . . ."

"Unless what?" asked the doctor.

"Unless they were—killed," whispered Paul.

Suddenly the smile left the doctor's eyes.

"Look!" cried Sandy, pointing to the ground

behind some plants. There lay the body of a dead cow. Dr. Lawrence looked the animal over. Its skin hung on its bones. On its neck were two tiny holes.

"Those holes must have been made by the teeth of a vampire bat!" cried Sandy.

"I don't think so," said her father. "Look how far apart the two holes are. The vampire bat is a very small animal. Its teeth are not so wide or so big."

"But no other animal would bite a cow in the neck and drink its blood," said Paul.

"No," said the doctor. "But a cow that gets a bat bite dies of disease. The bat drinks only a little of its blood. This cow didn't die of disease. It died because there isn't a drop of blood left in its body."

The young man's skin grew cold. "If a bat didn't drink this cow's blood, Doc, what did?" Paul asked.

A strange look came over Dr. Lawrence's face. "I don't know," he said slowly. "But I have an idea." Dr. Lawrence did not look at all happy now.

"I've only read about this in a book," Dr. Lawrence began. "Do you understand me? This may not be a true story, but by the looks of things here. . . . Well, I read about this small town in Transylvania. That's a place in Europe where they believe in vampire people. By day these vampires are dead in their graves. But at night they say they come out of their graves and attack humans. They drink their blood. The humans may die, but they are called the *undead*. At night they, too, come out of their graves and attack other humans. They become vampires. And their numbers grow."

"Oh, come on, Dad," said Sandy. "That's just

an old story. I read that book, too. It tells about how this one group of vampires got together and decided to take over the country. They wanted to turn everyone into vampires. But they never made it out of that town in Transylvania. People killed them for good in their coffins. They did it by driving stakes into their hearts. You don't think that kind of thing is really possible, do you?"

"As a man of science, I believe anything is possible. And the book I read says those vampires lie at peace in their graves. One of the vampires—the leader—is supposed to have escaped the stake. The story says that he still walks the earth, looking for new victims. That's what they believe in Transylvania."

"And that's what I believe," said Paul. Both Sandy and her father looked at him in surprise. "The holes we saw in that cow had to be made by human vampire teeth. And only a *human* vampire could drink that much blood."

CHAPTER **2**

## THE FIGHT

After the three Americans set up camp for the night, they got ready to sleep. Suddenly a loud scream broke through the dark night.

"What is it?" cried Dr. Lawrence.

"There's a man over there on the ground," Paul said, pointing to a spot close to camp. "It looks like some wild animal is on him." Paul reached for his gun.

"Be careful," said Dr. Lawrence. "You don't want to miss the animal and hit the man."

"You're right," answered Paul. He pointed the gun into the air and fired. He hoped the animal would be frightened away by the noise. The animal jumped up and let out a loud cry. The three campers could see its face in the light of the moon. It was not an animal at all, but a man. His mouth was full of sharp, pointed teeth. He looked up at Paul and the others. A wild look came into his eyes. He started toward them.

Dr. Lawrence now had his gun out too. Both he and Paul fired at the wild man, and the bullets hit their mark. The man stopped for a second in surprise. Then he looked down at where he had been hit and smiled.

"The bullets!" cried Sandy. "They didn't kill him! He's still coming!"

The two men fired again. A bullet hit the wild man right between the eyes. Another hit him in the stomach. But he kept right on walking toward them. He was only a few yards away from them now. They could clearly see his sharp teeth.

"Run!" cried Dr. Lawrence.

Paul threw his empty gun at the wild man and turned to run. His foot hit a plant and he fell. Sandy stopped to help him up. The man-animal was almost upon them.

Suddenly a loud beating of drums came from the village. The noise stopped the wild man in his tracks. He turned his head toward the drums. Then he looked back at Paul, Sandy, and the doctor. He waved a sharp rock in his hand. For a second it looked like he was going to throw it. But he didn't. Instead, he turned and ran toward the village.

"I hope he's gone for good," Sandy said. "Did you see those teeth? And why didn't he fall when he was shot?"

"The drums. . . ." whispered her father. "They seemed to be calling him away."

"Good for us," said Paul. "But look! Over there. The man he was fighting. He's moving."

CHAPTER **3**

# WORLD OF VAMPIRES

The three Americans rushed to the man's side. The man pulled away from them.

"It's all right," said the doctor. "We're your friends. I'm a doctor."

"No friends!" cried the man. "Only vampires!" He passed out.

"Human vampires. You were right, Dad," Sandy said.

"Yes, I'm sorry to say I was," said Dr. Lawrence. "But think of what this could mean for science. Come, Paul. Let's carry this man back to camp. We must ask him some questions."

Back at camp, Paul and Dr. Lawrence put the man into a sleeping bag and let him rest. In an hour he was awake. Sandy gave him some fruit to eat.

"Feel better now?" Dr. Lawrence asked him. "What's your name?"

"I feel better, yes, Doctor," answered the man. "My name is José. Thanks for saving my life."

"You can thank the drums for that," said Sandy. "If they hadn't called that creature away, we might *all* be dead now."

"The drums were an order to come to the village," José explained. His face showed worry. "The vampires were meeting in their nightly circle."

"What's all this talk about vampires?" said Dr. Lawrence. "Do you think we can believe such stories?"

José caught the doctor's shirt and pulled him toward him. There was a wild look in his eyes.

"You *must* believe," he said. "You must get away from here. We *all* must. Now!"

"But what about Taxacola?" asked Paul. "We've come to help the people. We *must* help them."

"There is no more Taxacola. There is only a village of vampires. Human vampires who live on the blood of animals and humans."

"Are you sure of that?" the doctor asked.

"I know all too well," said José. "I once lived in the village. All was well after you left us last time, Doctor. Then the cows started to die again. Then the people started to die too. Hernando was one of the first to die. He died right after dinner one night."

"Hernando is dead?" asked Dr. Lawrence.

"The man you knew as Hernando is dead, but a vampire is now in his body. Once Hernando died, he came back. Back to take others with him. He drank their blood and made them into vampires too. Soon there were only a few of us left alive. We could not leave our homes. The vampires were in every place. We had guns, but they were no use against these creatures."

"You're telling *me*!" Paul said.

"The only things they are afraid of are fire and a wooden stake through the heart. The stake is the only thing that will kill them. At night, we would make a ring of fire around the village to keep them out. By day, we would go looking for their resting place."

"Resting place?" asked Sandy.

"Yes. Vampires must sleep during the day. That is the only time they can be killed. One day I went looking for their resting place. I stayed out too long. When I got back to the village, it was already dark. The vampires had taken over the whole village. The village people are all vampires now. All but me."

"So all this time you have been out here, hiding from them," said Dr. Lawrence. "Why didn't you run away?"

"Because," said José, "my wife is one of them now. I must think of a way to save her. Maybe you can help me."

"If we could only find their resting place," Paul added.

"I have looked a long time and haven't found it," José said sadly.

"Then there's only one thing left to do," said Dr. Lawrence. "We'll have to let the vampires lead us to it. Let's get some rest. We're going vampire hunting at dawn."

# CHAPTER 4

## MAGDA

Dr. Lawrence woke up with the uneasy sense that someone was watching him. He opened his eyes. It was still dark. Then he recognized the tall figure leaning over his sleeping bag.

"Hernando!" cried Dr. Lawrence. His cry woke Sandy and Paul.

Hernando looked right at the doctor. His eyes were cold and mean. Dr. Lawrence saw that Hernando was not alone. Several villagers were standing behind him, watching.

"Why do you call me by my name?" Hernando asked. "I do not know you."

"Of course you know me!" cried the doctor. "I'm the man who saved your village from the vampire bats only a year ago. I'm sure you must remember. I'm Doctor Lawrence. This is my daughter, Sandy, and my helper, Paul Ross."

Hernando didn't look at the young people.

"Why have you come back to Taxacola?" he wanted to know.

"Because *you* asked me to come." Dr. Lawrence reached into his shirt pocket and pulled out a piece of paper. "Don't tell me you forget about writing this letter, too."

Hernando took the letter from the doctor's hand. He took a quick look at it and tore it into little pieces. He let the pieces fall to the ground.

"We do not need your help any more," he said. "We need more than that now. We need your blood." He grabbed Dr. Lawrence's arm.

Sandy gasped.

Dr. Lawrence shut his eyes. He was ready to die. But suddenly Hernando let go of him. He opened his eyes. The vampire leader was looking hard at Sandy. It seemed that he was seeing her for the first time. He was shaking. "Is it you, Magda?" Hernando said to Sandy. "Could it be you?"

Sandy thought fast. "Yes, it is me—Magda," she said. She would say anything if it would save her father.

"Oh, Magda. How? How did you find me?" Hernando suddenly looked weak. He saw that the sun was beginning to rise. He said, "I must go now. But I will come back for you soon, Magda."

Slowly the other vampires followed their leader back toward the village. José followed them.

"Father," said Sandy. "Are you all right?"

Dr. Lawrence rubbed his arm and smiled at his daughter. "Yes, yes, my dear," he said. "Thanks to you. And thanks to Magda."

"But who is this Magda?" Sandy asked. "Do you know?"

"Yes. I didn't remember until Hernando said her name. But let's not waste time. I'll tell you later. Now we must follow the vampires to their resting place."

They took off after the vampires. Soon they caught up with José. The three walked just far enough behind José so the creatures didn't see them. They climbed over hills and piles of broken rock. The sun was well up when they finally came to the opening of a large cave.

"Let's go in and see what vampires look like when they're sleeping," said Paul.

José stopped him. "We must wait until we're sure they are all asleep," he warned. "We don't want to be in their power again."

"José knows what he's talking about," said the doctor. "We'll wait."

A half-hour passed. No sound came from the cave. José spent the time cutting sharp points on pieces of dead wood to make stakes. As they waited, Sandy talked to Paul. Then she turned to her father. "Now tell me about this woman, Magda."

Dr. Lawrence smiled a minute and rubbed his beard. "I read about Magda in the book we talked about before. She was a young woman who lived in the small town in Transylvania. The leader of the vampire people fell in love with her. And she with him. They were going to get married in some strange ceremony. She was to become a vampire. But during the ceremony the people from the town came with stakes. All the vampires were killed. But the leader escaped. It seems he never saw Magda again —until now."

"Wait a minute," said Paul. "I'm not following you. Sandy isn't Magda, and Hernando isn't —isn't. . . ."

"Isn't the leader from Transylvania," added the doctor. "But he might think he's the vampire leader. Or maybe he really is. The leader could have come to Mexico and taken over Hernando's body. That doesn't matter. What matters is that he thinks my daughter is Magda. Magda had fair hair and—"

"Please don't, Dad. I don't want to hear it. Thinking about being close to Hernando makes me sick. And he said that he'll be back for me. That's OK in books—right? But this is too real."

"Maybe it would be better if you went home," the doctor told his daughter.

"Forget it," said Sandy. Her face grew strong. She looked right into her father's eyes. "I'm staying with you."

"That goes for me, too," said Paul.

Then José looked at Dr. Lawrence. "It is time," he said.

As they walked toward the cave entrance, Paul and Sandy talked.

"We now know that the human vampires killed the cows," said Paul.

"What we don't know is *how* the first humans became vampires," Sandy said.

Paul rubbed his head. "How did the villagers use their cows, José?"

"They used them for work in their fields."

"Anything else?"

"Well, sometimes they ate a few cows."

"That's it!" cried Sandy. "You said before that Hernando ate dinner before he suddenly died. He must have eaten cow meat. The meat was bad. It killed him."

"That still doesn't explain what made him into a vampire," said Paul.

"Save the talk for later," broke in Dr. Lawrence. "Let's see what's inside."

CHAPTER **5**
CAVE OF THE DEAD|

José picked up a torch from behind a rock and lit it so they could see their way. Then the four people went into the cave.

After they had walked for a while, Dr. Lawrence said, "The cave is opening up into some kind of room."

The torch threw light into the new room. In it were large stone coffins. A damp smell like rain came through the close air of the cave.

"It is the Cave of the Dead," whispered José.

"What's that?" asked Sandy.

"The place where the dead people of the village used to be put many years ago," explained José. "No one has been here for a long time."

"A good place for vampires to hide out," said Dr. Lawrence.

"Look!" cried Sandy, pointing to a spot nearby. A large pile of human bones lay in the corner of the cave.

"What are they doing there?" asked Paul.

"When the vampires wanted to use the coffins, they had to clear the bones out," said the doctor. "Let's have a look. Try to pull off the top of one of these coffins."

José put the torch in a crack in the wall. Then he and Paul took the top off the biggest coffin. It was very heavy and took several minutes to take off. Inside the coffin was Hernando. His eyes were closed. His skin was soft and white, like a baby's. A thin line of blood ran down from his mouth.

"He is the leader," said José. "It is best we start with him."

"Start *what*?" asked Sandy.

José lifted one of his wooden stakes and put the sharp point over Hernando's heart. With his free hand he picked up a rock. He was ready to pound the stake through the vampire's heart.

"No!" cried Dr. Lawrence suddenly.

José jumped back from the coffin. "What's the matter?" he asked.

"You can't kill them like this!" cried Dr. Lawrence. "It isn't their fault they've become vampires."

"Then whose fault is it?" Sandy asked.

The doctor covered his face with his hands. "It's my fault," he cried. "All my fault."

"Dad, what are you saying?"

"It's clear to me now," he answered. "You were right, Sandy. It *was* the cow meat that did it. The cow meat that Hernando ate. The meat with *my* serum in it!"

"But how could that change them into vampires?" Paul asked.

"Part of the serum was taken from the blood of bats. The serum killed the bats when they drank the blood. Then the blood in the cow's veins infected the meat. The humans who ate the meat died. And turned into vampires."

"So that's it," said José slowly. "*You* did it. *You* made the village of vampires. *You* took my wife from me." He looked at the fire of the torch.

Dr. Lawrence's mouth made a thin line. "Maybe I can make another serum that will save the village people. A serum that will bring them back to life as humans," he said to José. "At least I can try. Now put the top on that coffin, and let's go. I must get to work."

"I just hope you know what you're doing *this* time, Doctor," said José.

Paul and José put the heavy lid back on the coffin. Then Paul took up the torch and started to lead the way out of the cave. Suddenly his foot hit a rock. The torch fell from his hand. It landed in a small pool of water and went out. At once the cave was as black as night.

"Where is everyone?" called Sandy.

"I can't see a thing," Paul said.

"It's all right," said Dr. Lawrence. "Everyone stay cool, and nothing will happen. Join hands. . . . Everyone together?" the doctor asked at last.

"Yes." The three voices made a ringing sound in the darkness.

"All right. Let's go ahead. But very slowly."

As they moved to the opening of the cave, José stopped short.

"What's the matter?" asked Paul.

"That noise. . . ." whispered José.

"What noise?" said Sandy. "I don't hear a thing."

"It's like wings beating against the air," José said.

"Yes," said Dr. Lawrence. "I hear it now."

The noise grew louder.

"It sounds like birds flying through the cave," said Paul.

"No, not birds," whispered the doctor. "Probably *bats*."

"What kind of bats?" asked Sandy with a shudder.

"Only vampire bats live around here," her father answered. "And I thought I had seen the last of them."

Suddenly Paul's voice shook the cave. "A bat hit me in the head!"

"Run!" cried Dr. Lawrence. "They're after our blood!" He pushed the three others in front of him.

They ran, covering their heads with their arms. Soon they saw light through the opening in the cave.

"Get out of the cave!" cried the doctor. "The bats won't follow us into the light. Hurry!"

In another minute, Sandy, Paul, and José fell to the ground outside the cave, breathing hard.

"That was a close call!" Paul said. "Anyone hurt?"

"I got a small bite on my hand," said José. "But it's not bad."

Sandy was looking around wildly. "Where's my father?" she asked.

"I don't know," said José. "I thought he was following us."

"He's not out here," said Paul, after looking around. "He must still be inside the cave."

"Come on," said José, getting to his feet. "We've got to find him." They ran back into the cave.

"Dr. Lawrence! Dad!" Their voices trailed off into the darkness. There was no answer. Even the bats had gone.

"Dad," cried Sandy loudly. "Can't you hear us?"

"Help," cried a voice that was far away.

"Dr. Lawrence, where are you?" said Paul. He walked ahead of Sandy and José.

"Down here," answered the voice.

Just then Paul's right foot kicked a rock. He heard the rock land somewhere far below. There was a deep hole in the floor of the cave. Paul looked down into the black hole. With the light from the cave entrance he could just make out Dr. Lawrence's face looking up at him.

"Help me!" the doctor cried. He was standing on a weak ledge. The rock was starting to give way.

"Give me your hand!" Paul cried, reaching down to him.

The doctor reached up as far as he could. But

it was not far enough. "I can't reach you," he said.

Paul looked around for a stick to hold out to the doctor. But there was no stick in the cave. In a few seconds Dr. Lawrence would drop.

CHAPTER **6**

## JOSÉ, THE *UNDEAD*

Sandy was by Paul's side now. "Paul, why don't you and José lower me into the hole?" she said. "Then I'll be able to reach Dad's hand and pull him up."

"Good idea," said José. "I just hope we're strong enough." He and Paul took hold of Sandy's legs and lowered her several feet into the hole.

Sandy grabbed the doctor by his arms.

"Got him?" cried José. "We can't hold on much longer."

Slowly José and Paul pulled Sandy and Dr. Lawrence up out of the hole and onto the cave floor.

"Thank you all," said the doctor, "I could feel my life slipping away. But I'm OK now. Let's get out of this ugly cave."

Outside, he checked everyone's bumps and scratches.

"Your hand, José," said the doctor. "There's blood on it."

"Just a small bite from one of those bats," said José.

"Small bite nothing," said the doctor. "You could get sick from it." José said nothing. The doctor knew that José blamed him for the terror of the vampires. Little could José know how the doctor blamed himself.

As soon as they got back to camp, Dr. Lawrence cleaned and covered José's cut. Then he set to work.

From his bag he took several books, two brown bottles, and many little boxes. Then he cleared a small place to work.

"I thought all the vampire bats were killed off by your first serum, Doc," said Paul.

"So did I," said Dr. Lawrence as he opened a bottle. "But it seems a few lived. They must have been too strong for the serum to kill."

"Strong enough to go after humans and turn them into vampires, too," said Sandy suddenly.

Her father turned to her. "What are you saying?" he asked.

"I'm saying that I don't think it was your serum in the cows' meat that did it," she said. "It was the bats. They turned Taxacola into a village of vampires."

"But most of the time vampire bats don't come after people," said the doctor. "I just don't understand it."

"Well, they sure did a good job in the cave," answered Paul. "They bit José. Hey, where is José?"

The doctor was not listening. "If José turns into a vampire, we'll know it was the bats that caused the trouble. Not my serum," he said, almost to himself. "But if he turns into a vampire, we've got to save him."

"Dad," said Sandy. "Where did José go?"

"I don't know," said Dr. Lawrence. "You and Paul had better look for him."

Sandy and Paul walked away from camp on different paths. It was nearly dark. Soon Sandy saw a large flat rock in an open space. José was lying on the rock with his arms and legs stretched out.

"What are you doing?" Sandy asked him.

José looked up at her and smiled. "I am watching the night come," he said.

"Father would like to see you," Sandy told him.

"I thought he was making serum," answered José.

"He is. And it may have been the bats, not the serum, that made your people vampires," Sandy said. "That bite might turn *you* into a vampire."

José laughed. "Might? It *has*!"

"It's nothing to joke about, José," Sandy said. But suddenly she knew why he was talking that way. With the coming of night, José was no longer human. José was becoming one of the *undead*.

Suddenly drums started beating.

Sandy covered her ears with her hands. "Those drums make my blood run cold," she said. "José, why are they beating?"

"They are calling one of their brothers," said José in a soft voice. "They are sending him a message from the vampire leader. They are ordering him to do something. Something that should have been done a long time ago."

"What is it that the leader wants him to do?"

"He wants him to take a young woman away from her father. He wants him to bring her to him."

José turned his head toward Sandy. His eyes were changed. They were cold and mean. Just like Hernando's eyes. He stood up.

"José, you're one of them now, aren't you?" Sandy asked. She backed away.

"I am your friend," answered José, holding out his hand. "I will not hurt you. Look into my eyes. Look into my eyes and rest. Rest until you wake up at the Feast of the Dead. On the night you and Hernando will be married."

Sandy tried to look away. But it was no use. She couldn't take her eyes from José's. Suddenly she was in a deep trance.

"Come, Sandy," he said softly. "Hernando and the others wait in the village." They stood up together.

Paul came running up to them. "Sandy," he cried. "What's going on?"

When Sandy turned to look at him, his heart almost missed a beat. "Go away," she said in a cold voice. "Leave us alone."

Paul grabbed her by the arms. "Sandy. What's happened to you?"

"She's coming with me," José said. When he opened his mouth, Paul could see the long, sharp teeth of a vampire.

"You—you're one of them," Paul said. It was hard for him to believe it. "The vampire bat *did* make you a vampire."

"Yes, it did. Now go back and tell your doctor to stop worrying. Tell him to leave us alone. We don't need his cure."

Paul reached out to hit José. But suddenly everything went black, and Paul fell.

When he came to, Dr. Lawrence was standing over him.

"Paul, what happened? Where's Sandy?"

"José has taken her away to the vampires. He's one of them. Someone hit me over the head. It must have been Sandy. She was standing right behind me."

"Are you out of your mind? Why would she do a thing like that?"

"She wasn't herself," Paul answered. "José put her into some kind of trance. She's in his power. There's no time to lose. We've got to go after them at once."

Dr. Lawrence grabbed Paul's arm. "Wait a minute, Paul," he said. "José is probably back in the village by now. We can't fight them all. You saw what happened before. They'd kill us before we could get near Sandy. It's probably better to wait until morning—when they're back in the cave asleep."

"But what about Sandy?" cried Paul.

"If they think she's Magda, she should be safe. And Paul, I've just made a serum that could make every vampire a human again! It will protect us all!"

# CHAPTER 7
## DANCE OF DEATH

Sandy was in a trance. Her face showed no feelings. She sat in the middle of a circle of vampires. The sound of drums, like the beating of bats' wings, was all around her. Hernando and José watched the young woman.

"It is almost time," José said to Hernando. He looked hungry. "Her blood must be very sweet."

"We will feast when I say so," said Hernando. "First, we must go through the ceremony as it was done in the old country. The ceremony is important. It will bring more blood."

Suddenly Hernando lifted his arms toward the dark sky. He looked like he wanted to reach for the moon. The whole group of vampires did the same thing. They looked at Sandy with their black eyes.

Then Sandy also lifted her arms. She stood

up as the drums grew very loud. Her still face was as beautiful as a flower.

The drums stopped. Suddenly Sandy screamed. Her scream rang through the empty houses of the village. It rang through the cold night air and out among the rocks.

"Scream, Magda," Hernando said in a strong voice. "Scream for this village of vampires. You are the one with blood as clear as a mountain stream. Blood that will make us strong."

A great cry went up around the circle.

Yes, thought José. This is good.

"Yes," screamed the vampires. "Yes! Blood that will make us strong!"

Hernando's arms made circles in the air. So did the arms of the other vampires. All the vampires began a strange dance around Sandy. As they danced, the circle around her slowly got very small. Soon Hernando stood next to Sandy and looked into her eyes. He asked her a question in a soft voice.

"You know what you are here for, don't you, Magda? You know why you came to me?"

Sandy turned to face Hernando. She was quiet.

Hernando asked her again. "Magda, do you know why you are here?"

"Yes," said Sandy. Her voice was very low.

"What are you going to do, Magda?"

"I will become a vampire," she said.

"She will become a vampire," shouted all the others.

"I will become Hernando's wife," she said, louder than before.

"She will become Hernando's wife," chanted the vampire villagers.

"I will drink the blood of humans!" Sandy screamed.

"She will drink the blood of humans!" screamed all those in the circle.

"Oh, that is so good, Magda. Everything is so clear." Hernando was speaking now. "You want to be a vampire very soon, don't you? You want to be with us and drink the sweet, red milk we need so much."

A big smile came to Sandy's face. Her golden hair was as bright as fire. The circle of vampires around Hernando and Sandy grew even smaller. Many hands reached out toward her. Sandy shook her head wildly so that her hair stood out. But she was not afraid.

Then Hernando said in a loud voice, "Now it is time. Magda will become one of us. She will become my wife in a living death. Let us sing."

All the vampires began to sing. The music filled the village. José and his vampire wife reached out and took Sandy's arms.

They led Sandy toward a large pole and put her against it. Then José took out a knife. The *undead* crowded around the pole.

Then Hernando broke through the crowd. "Wait," he said. "The morning light is coming."

Suddenly the sky in the east grew bright. The sun was coming up. The vampires had forgotten about the coming of day.

"Back to the cave!" Hernando shouted. "Fast! Everyone back!"

Dr. Lawrence and Paul spent a night without sleep. By the first light of morning, they were ready to look for Sandy. Dr. Lawrence poured the serum he had made into many bottles. Then he carefully put them into his pack.

"What are you packing, Paul?" the doctor asked.

"Wooden stakes," Paul answered. "I'm bringing them along just in case your serum doesn't work."

Dr. Lawrence shuddered. "Let's hope we never have to use them," he said.

"Come," said Paul. "We have no time to lose."

Before the sun was very high in the sky, they reached the cave—or what they thought was the cave.

"That's strange," Paul said. "There's no opening here. We must have lost our way."

Dr. Lawrence kicked the rocks at the foot of the mountain and shook his head. "No, we didn't get lost," he said. "This is the opening to the cave all right. These rocks are loose. There is no dirt around them. That means they fell just a short time ago. They closed off the opening. José knew we would come after him. He and the other vampires must have started a rock slide so we couldn't get in."

Paul picked up a rock and threw it into the pile. "It would take us a year to dig through and get inside."

"There must be another way in," Dr. Lawrence said. "If there wasn't, how could the vampires get out again?"

"You're right, Doc! But can we find it before the sun sets once more?" asked Paul.

"We'll *have* to!"

They climbed the hills around the cave and looked for another opening. For hours they looked everywhere. But they found nothing. "It's no use," said Paul. "We'll never find the other opening. We might as well give up."

"Not on your life!" said Dr. Lawrence. "There has to be a way. Let me think some more."

After a while, a smile lit Dr. Lawrence's face. "Why didn't we think of it before, Paul?" he said.

"Think of what?"

"A sure way to find our way into the cave. Follow the bats! Follow the bats into the cave!"

CHAPTER **8**

## STOPPING THE VAMPIRES

"Of course," shouted Dr. Lawrence. He was almost jumping up and down. "Why didn't I think of that before? In the morning we'll follow the bats and find the way into the cave."

"But what about the vampires?" Paul asked. "Wouldn't they be easier to follow? And by morning it may be too late for Sandy."

"No, it's too hard to follow them at night. They can see in the dark—we can't. Remember, now, we don't have José to lead us. They would catch us for sure. But in the early morning our eyes are better than theirs." The doctor no longer looked tired and old. He took hold of Paul's arm and grinned his happy grin. "As for tonight, we can make sure that the vampires leave my daughter alone."

A questioning look passed over Paul's face. "But how can we pull that off?"

"With garlic, my good man, garlic!" shouted the doctor.

He's gone crazy, Paul thought. But the doctor talked on.

"I knew I forgot one thing that vampires were afraid of, but I couldn't think of it until tonight. Garlic! And look! We're standing in a whole field of it now! Pull up all you can carry, Paul. Hurry. Sandy's life may depend on this garlic."

Paul took off his shirt and used it to hold many plants. He put a small torch he had brought from the camp in the shirt before he tied it up. "Now what, Doc?" he asked.

The doctor waved in the direction of the vampire village. "You'll see. Let's get going."

When the two men got to the village, they saw a woman vampire. She was standing watch over the sacred poles.

"How about running down there?" the doctor whispered to Paul. "Give me the garlic. Then let that vampire see you, and take off. When she follows you, run around for about five minutes. Then lead her back to their sacred poles. By that time, I should have put garlic all over them."

Paul walked toward the poles, let the woman see him, and then started running. The vampire went after him. Right away Dr. Lawrence picked up the garlic and ran to the sacred poles. Tearing pieces from Paul's shirt, he tied all but two plants to the poles. The smell of garlic filled the air.

When Paul came running back into the village, the vampire was close behind. Paul reached the doctor and stopped. The vampire stopped too, a few feet from the men. She saw the garlic and jumped back in surprise. Then she ran away, screaming.

"Good job," said the doctor. "Now she will go to Hernando. Soon every vampire in Mexico will be here."

Paul looked at the garlic-hung poles. "What a smell," he said. "I never could stand garlic. Now I love it!"

"Quick," said Dr. Lawrence. "Let's get behind those rocks and see what happens."

Soon Hernando and the other vampires rushed into the village. They all stopped when they saw the garlic.

All night, Paul and Dr. Lawrence watched the vampires try many ways to save their sacred poles. They kicked dirt at them. They tried to throw blankets over them. But the vampires were too afraid. They could not get close enough to the poles to do any good. A short time before the sun came up, the vampires returned to their cave.

When it started to get light, Paul and the doctor went toward the mountain. They had two garlic plants in their packs.

As they walked, Dr. Lawrence spoke. "If I live through the next few days," he said, "I can give the Mexicans my two serums. One for killing vampire bats. And the new one for bringing back human life to vampire people. But if I die you must make sure that my formulas are not lost."

"Somehow," said Paul, "we will all live through this. I just know we will."

"Look!" Dr. Lawrence pointed up at the mountain. A group of black creatures were flying down into the foot of it.

"Vampire bats!" cried Paul. "The other opening to the cave must be there."

"Yes," answered the doctor. "Quick! We must get to it." The two men raced across the rocks to the mountain. They moved as though they had new power. Paul got there first. He saw a black hole below him. "This is it!" he cried.

"Watch out for the bats!" Dr. Lawrence shouted behind him. "We must light the torch."

The way down into the cave didn't look easy. There was nothing to hold on to.

"We'll have to use our stakes." Paul was speaking. "We can stick them into the cracks in the rocks and hold on to them. But we'll have to pull them back out as we go down."

"Great idea!" said the doctor. He threw a stone into the hole. They heard it land not too far below.

Paul went down first. He placed a stake in between two rocks. "Be careful!" he called, as he lowered himself with the stakes. "Let yourself down easy."

But the doctor should have been more careful. As he got down on his knees to step into the hole, the pack slipped off his back. By this time Paul was on the floor of the cave.

"The serum!" cried Paul, looking up. But it was too late. He could not catch the pack and hold the torch at the same time. The pack hit the rocks on the cave floor with a loud smashing of glass. Paul rushed over to it. The cave floor was wet. Only one bottle of serum was left unbroken. He handed it to Dr. Lawrence as the doctor reached the cave's floor.

"For Sandy," he said.

"And for the rest," said the doctor slowly, "the wooden stake."

In a few minutes they stood in the room where the vampires were sleeping. The stone coffins were just as they had been before.

"There's not a minute to waste," said Dr. Lawrence. "We've got to find her." He took the torch and set it in a crack in the wall. Then he began lifting the heavy coffin tops. Paul helped him. Suddenly they stopped when they looked into one special coffin. Tears rolled down the doctor's face as he looked inside. Sandy was lying there. Her lips were parted. She was dressed all in white. Her eyes were shut.

The doctor shook Sandy with both arms. "Wake up, Sandy! Wake up!" But she didn't move. It was as if she were dead.

Dr. Lawrence finally let her down into the coffin again. "There are no marks on her neck," he said in a quiet voice.

Then he lifted a wooden stake from his pack.

He turned to the open coffin next to Sandy's. Hernando lay inside it.

Dr. Lawrence pointed a shaking finger at the vampire's white face. "Look," he said. "The creature is smiling. He thinks she is all his now." He handed the stake to Paul.

"You do it," Dr. Lawrence said." I don't want to touch him."

Paul lifted a rock from the floor and put the sharp end of the stake over Hernando's heart. He pulled back the hand holding the rock. "May you stay dead forever!" he cried. He hit the stake hard with the rock.

The stake went into the vampire's chest. Hernando opened his eyes. He screamed. It was a frightening sound. Paul drove the stake in again. Hernando screamed again, louder this time. Paul stepped away and dropped the rock. He put his hands over his ears. He couldn't stand the sound any more.

The vampire's hands grabbed the stake, madly trying to pull it out. But it was too late.

Dr. Lawrence picked up the rock and moved up to the coffin. He continued pounding the stake. Suddenly there was a sound of breaking wood. The stake broke against the bottom of the coffin. It had gone clear through Hernando's body. The vampire stopped screaming, and his hands let go of the stake. His eyes closed again as a peaceful look washed over his face.

"He is dead at last," said the doctor. "*Really* dead. Come. We must finish off the others before it is dark. You take one side and I'll take the other. Make sure the stake goes through the heart. That's the only way to really kill them."

Paul picked up a stake. It felt very cold in his hands. He looked at the sleeping vampire in the next coffin and shuddered. Could he do it again? Before, he had thought he could kill Hernando, but he had had to stop. Now, he looked at the vampires before him. They were asleep and helpless. He wasn't so sure he could even start.

"What are you waiting for?" asked Dr. Lawrence. He was about to stake another vampire. "We must work quickly."

Paul shook his head to clear it. He put the stake in place and went to work. He moved on to the next coffin and did it again. One by one, the two men finished off the sleeping vampires. The walls of the cave rang with their last screams. But Paul's ears were dead to them now. He only thought of Sandy in her deathlike sleep.

Would the death of the vampires remove Sandy from their hold? Only time would tell. There was now only one vampire left to stake. Paul looked into the stone coffin. It was José. José—who had once been as human as Paul was. José—whose life they had saved. Now Paul was about to take that same life away. He put the last stake in place over José's heart. He lifted the rock in his hand, wet with blood.

Suddenly José's eyes opened. He looked up at Paul. The rock shook in Paul's hand as José started to sit up. José's hand reached for Paul's neck. The rock fell to the floor.

CHAPTER **9**
## DEAD EYES

José's hand pressed Paul's neck. When Paul let out a half cry, the doctor turned around.

"So, you were going to destroy us, were you?" said José. His eyes showed a spark of hate. "Well, the sun has set and our powers have returned. Now it will be our turn to destroy *you*."

"You are all alone now, José," said Dr. Lawrence. "All your friends are dead, even Hernando." The doctor's voice was cracked and weak. He had worked very hard, and he was an old man.

José turned his head and looked around. The sight of the dead vampires surprised him. He let go of Paul's neck for a second. This was just the opening Paul needed. He pulled away from the vampire and ran for his pack on the floor. Get the garlic, he thought. But there was no time.

José turned back to Paul and let out an animal cry. He climbed out of the coffin and came at Paul. Paul backed up against the cave wall.

José was almost on him when Dr. Lawrence threw a rock. The rock made a deep cut in José's head. He didn't bleed. But he sang out an ugly scream and turned on Dr. Lawrence. The doctor threw another rock and hit José in the leg. The vampire jumped on him, knocking him to the ground.

Paul looked up and saw the torch set into the wall. Fire—the other thing vampires were afraid of!

He took down the torch and waved the flame in José's face. The vampire let the doctor go at once. Paul waved the fire at him again. José jumped up and moved away.

Paul moved the vampire back into the cave with the torch. José tried to knock the torch out of Paul's hand, but he was too afraid of the flames.

"Paul, put that thing down. I won't hurt you. Just let me go," José said. He fell to the ground. He looked like an animal in a trap.

"How do I know you mean what you say?" Paul answered.

"I was your friend, remember? I can be your

friend again, Paul. Why not put down the torch?"

José's eyes grew larger and larger. Paul couldn't help looking into them. He's putting me into a trance, Paul thought. Just like he did with Sandy.

"That's right, Paul," José said softly. "Keep looking into my eyes and drop the torch."

Paul shut his eyes. "Never!" he cried. "Death to all vampires!"

He touched the torch to José's shirt. It caught on fire. The vampire fell down, wildly trying to put out the flames. But the fire burned him quickly. When José stopped moving, Paul went up and put a stake through his heart. Through the cave, all was quiet.

Paul turned and slowly walked back to where Dr. Lawrence lay.

"The last vampire is dead," Paul said quietly.

"No," answered the doctor. "There's still one left." The old man held out a shaking hand. The last bottle of serum rolled between his fingers.

"Here," Dr. Lawrence whispered. "Give this to Sandy. Quickly, I want to know my daughter is all right before . . . before. . . ."

"Before what?"

The eyes in Dr. Lawrence's head went dead. "Before you must kill me," he said.

CHAPTER **10**

## WHO GETS THE SERUM?

Paul's mouth fell open. He could say nothing. "Kill you?" he said at last. "Are you mad?"

"No," answered the doctor in a sad voice. "I only wish I were. Before you got to José with the torch, he bit me. It's not a bad bite. But it's bad enough. See?" He held out a bloody hand.

"The sun has set," he went on. "Any minute now I may become a blood-drinking vampire like José and the others. You must kill me the same way you did them. You must do it now, before I hurt you."

"But the serum!" Paul cried. "The serum can save you!"

"There is only enough serum for one person. You *must* give it to Sandy. Do you hear me? Give it to her now."

Paul turned to Sandy's coffin and took her in his arms. "Sandy! Wake up!" he cried, shaking her. "Show your father you're all right. Show him you're not a vampire." Sandy's head began to move.

"Hernando. . . ." she whispered through cold lips.

Paul shook her even more. "Sandy! It's Paul. Hernando's dead. He can't hurt you any more. You're free."

"What are you waiting for?" the doctor said. "Give her the serum!"

"Tonight. . . ." Sandy whispered. "Tonight I will join them for the feast. The Feast of the Dead!"

"No." Paul kept at it. "There will be no feast. It's all over."

Sandy's eyes opened slowly. They were glassy, not mean and cold. They looked the way they had when Paul first saw her under José's spell. He knew at once she was still in a trance. He snapped his fingers, then clapped his hands. Slowly the glassy look left her eyes.

"Paul," she said in a weak voice. "Where am I? What am I doing here?"

"She's all right, Doc!" Paul shouted. "She's not a vampire. They were saving that for tonight. Do you hear me, Doc?"

But from the dark side of the cave there came no answer. Paul reached down into the pack and pulled out a needle. He filled it with serum. Then he took out a garlic plant.

"Father!" Sandy said. "Where are you?"

Out of the darkness came a low cry. It was more animal than human.

"What's happened to my father?" Sandy asked.

"He'll be all right," Paul whispered softly. "Stay here. Don't move. I'm going to inject him with the serum."

Paul moved into the darkness, the needle in one hand.

"Come out, Dr. Lawrence," he called. "I'm going to give you the serum now. I want to help make you well. Please come out."

Suddenly there was a wild cry. Two arms grabbed Paul from behind. The needle fell from his hand, but he held onto the garlic. The arms pushed him to the ground. He looked up into the face of his friend, the man he worked for. The doctor's eyes were cold and mean. They were the eyes of a vampire.

The cold hands closed in on him. The sharp teeth came down toward his neck. Paul pushed the garlic in the doctor's face.

Then the hands suddenly let go. The wild
look went out of Dr. Lawrence's eyes. He fell
forward onto Paul. Paul pushed him off. He
could see the needle sticking out of the doctor's
arm. Sandy stood before him.

"Are you all right?" she asked. "I picked up
the needle and gave Dad the shot as fast as I
could."

Paul lay on the floor, rubbing his neck. "Talk

about close calls!" he said. "I'm OK, Sandy. It's a good thing you came out here after us. Now let's see about your dad."

Sandy looked at her father. He seemed to be asleep. "I wonder how long it will take for the serum to work."

Paul pulled the empty needle from the doctor's arm. "We'll just have to wait and see."

A few minutes passed. Then Dr. Lawrence opened his eyes. "Paul. Sandy. What happened?"

Paul smiled. "For a minute, you were growing long teeth," he said.

A week later, Paul, Sandy, and Dr. Lawrence were sitting down for dinner in Paul's apartment in the United States.

Paul still looked a little tired. But he had fixed a great spaghetti dinner for his friends. This was their first get-together since they had come back from Mexico. They had rested for a whole week. But, even with rest, their lives would never be the same.

They talked for a while about their narrow escape in Mexico—about José, Hernando, the whole village of vampires. Sandy told her father and Paul that she would never again go into another cave. Then they sat down to eat.

"Paul," said Sandy. "Your spaghetti sauce is good. Does it have garlic in it? I didn't think you liked garlic."

"Oh, but he does now," joked Dr. Lawrence. "He likes it best at night!"